THE PEBBLE FALL THEME PARK

Welcome to the Pebble Fall Theme Park

KEERTIGA CHANDRAN

PARTRIDGE

Print information available on the last page.

To order additional copies of this book, contact
Toll Free 800 101 2657 (Singapore)
Toll Free 1 800 81 7340 (Malaysia)
orders.singapore@partridgepublishing.com

www.partridgepublishing.com/singapore

FOR MY MOM, THANK YOU SO MUCH FOR
THE FINANCIAL SUPPORT, FOR LENDING ME
MONEY WHEN I ASKED YOU IN THE BEGINNING
OF MY NOVEL PUBLISHING CAREER.

WHAT'S UP, SWEETHEARTS? FIRST OF ALL, WANNA LET YOU GUYS KNOW THAT NO MATTER WHO YOU ARE AND WHERE YOU COME FROM, YOU ARE BEAUTIFUL. KEEP SMILING AND CHEER UP, BEAUTIFUL AND HANDSOME.:]]]]] – AUTHOR'S NOTE.

THE CHARACTERS CAST IDEAS WERE INSPIRED FROM THE AUTHOR, AUTHOR'S FRIEND AND SEVERAL CELEBRITIES.

- **Keertiga Chandran** as **Keertiga Chandran**
- **Lily Collins** as **Nina Parrish**
- **Thurgashini Nair Ragawan** as **Shini Johnson**
- **Grant Gustin** as **Gustin Collins**
- **Taylor Lautner** as **Jacob Watson**
- **Colton Parrish** as **Colton Evans**

I WOULD LIKE THANK LILY COLLINS, GRANT GUSTIN, TAYLOR LAUTNER AND COLTON PARRISH FOR UNKNOWINGLY BECOMING A PART OF MY NOVEL.

CONTENTS

CHAPTER 1

ROCKHURST

The song 'Dollhouse' by Melanie Martinez filled the van as we were on our way to the countryside of Rockhurst. We were all in 7th heaven delight as this was our first business trip together.......never knowing what was going to happen next. Gustin, Colton, Jacob, Nina, Shini and I had planned to hugely renovate the abandoned theme park in Rockhurst to become an eco-theme park. The former Pebble Fall Theme Park which was originally opened in 1965 drawing upwards of 8000 visitors a day-was still intact, but became abandoned due to the fire accident on the wheel rider which killed six children and one adult and the death of a 10-year old boy in the water ride. The reason behind these tragic incidents were mysterious. Since we were all school leavers, half of the fund was supplied by Mr. Alex's company, who was Gustin's father. Our one month stay in Rockhurst would basically be taken care by the company itself.

In the van, Colton focused on the road while driving. Meanwhile, the rest of us were trying to soak up as much Vitamin D as possible. Talking about me, I'm Keertiga Chandran and I was one of the few brown girls in the United States. I had a wavy dark brown hair with a tall skinny figure. My skin looked pale against the sunshine. Regardless,the greatest being the palest from all of us was my boyfriend,Gustin. I looked at Gustin whom already had his eyes on me. I reached my hand out and stroked his left cheek, looking into his eyes. Gustin's beautiful blue eyes would glow whenever he was under the Sun. He smiled my favourite crooked smile. Gustin was a whole new brand of perfection. Flinching away from my overwhelming thought, I smirked then leaned in to give him a peck on the lips. He then short kissed me back, knowing that we're not the only lovebirds in the van. Nina and Colton were together as well, same went to Shini and Jacob. The two lovebirds at front were having their very own moment with their hands intertwined. Even though I was glad for them, deep inside I was actually hoping that Colton wouldn't turn us out to appear on tomorrow's newspaper headlines.

The sun shone down and everything looked bright and holiday like. Cottages clustered together here and there and cattles grazed in the field. We soon arrived at one of Mr Alex's guesthouses. It was a comfortable looking house, painted in soft grey, set in a nice big garden. The moment Colton parked in front of the house, I could see a man, probably in his early 50's waving at us outside the house. After getting out of the van, Gustin then shook hands with the man. "Welcome to the Rockhurst, Gustin. Glad to see you all here!" The man said. "Hello Sir." All of us said smiling. He shook hands with all of us. The man uttered, "Okay, so let me introduce myself first. I'm Mr Lorenzo, Mr Alex's assistant manager. And yes, I will be taking care of your month needs in Rockhurst. So, come on in kids. Keep yourselves home. I'm living just a stone's threw away from here. So if you guys need anything, just give a call." "Thank you Mr Lorenzo. It is nice for you to come and welcome us." I expressed smiling. He then added, "Anytime dear." He smiled.

The boys then loaded our suitcases down from the boot and we all went into the house. Nina stated, "I have a funny feeling about this business trip, you know." Shini and I gave her a surprised look. "What do you mean, girl?" I hummed in Justin Bieber's 'What Do You Mean' tune. "I don't really know. But I've got a feeling. You girls just wait and see." Nina claimed. "Well, if it's funny in a good way, then I hope your feeling is right!" Shini commented and we all went into our rooms.

I had the sense that I had been asleep for a very long time. I inhaled deeply. Something familiar then touched my lips with the softest pressure. I opened my eyes and found the love of my life, smiling at me. His lips just half an inch from mine.

"Wake up sleepyhead." Gustin voiced smiling. I then smiled and pressed my lips softly against his. "Good morning, love." I stretched then yawned. I set myself up. I could feel his eyes on me. Gustin said, "It's not morning yet, love. It's just 6 in the evening. Mr Lorenzo might be here in any seconds to give us brief explanation, whatever related to

Pebble Fall theme park." He then stroked my hair. "Get ready fast. Jacob and Shini got us all food." He handed me my towel. I had always been grateful for having Gustin in my life. Mine and his relationship grew out of friendship. To be frank, he meant the world to me. He and I both knew that we could not live without each other. Meeting him at school was fate, becoming his friend was a choice, but falling in love with him was beyond my control. Being in love with your best friend is the greatest feeling in the world. Flinching away from my thoughts, I flickered my gaze towards Gustin, who was now standing in front of me. "Still in Disneyland?" he joked with a grin. I smirked then replied, "Why wouldn't I when I'm with the love of my life?" I held his face and pulled in for a long kiss.

Dinner was ready when Gustin and I got down holding hands. I was in khaki shorts and dark blue blouse. My hair was pulled into ponytail. Downstairs, round the table, I could see my homies including Mr Lorenzo, chattering nineteen to the dozen about everything, telling each other about their news, except Shini. Shini smiled as she listened, and handed round the plates of chicken and broccoli stir - fry. The smell amused me. Shini had been the best cook among all of us. I voiced, "What's up homies? Hello, Mr Lorenzo." I gave Mr Lorenzo a one - armed hug. "Hello, my dear." Mr Lorenzo responded. Gustin pulled out a chair for me and set himself next. The smell of the dish was mouth - watering, that I popped in one of the chickens into my mouth. "Mmm... Delicious." I muttered. "I do like these dish of yours Shini. They're the nicest I've ever tasted." Mr Lorenzo clarified. Nina added, "Yes indeed." She popped in more chickens. "Anyone would think you hadn't had anything to eat since breakfast - time, baby." Colton said. Nina jolted her lips out, "Well, we did have a good lunch before coming here. But that seems ages ago now." After we had done eating, we started our discussion as planned.

Mr Lorenzo took a thick book, which seemed old from his bag and set it on the front table in the living room. All of us surrounded the mighty table. He skipped a few pages front. We listened attentively. Mr Lorenzo spoke, "I'm sure Mr Alex has already given you guys a little explanation regarding the history of this theme park of ours. The 1965's famous Pebble Fall Theme Park was abandoned due to the fire accident on the Wheel Rider. Not only that, but a boy was killed in the Dibo's Water Ride. "Which killed 6 children and an adult." I added under my breath, thoughtfully, thinking Mr Lorenzo wouldn't hear but no, I was wrong. "That's right." Mr Lorenzo said.

"And the reason behind the fire accident is unidentified." Jacob stated thoughtfully. Mr Lorenzo responded, "Ahem." He nodded. "In its heyday, the theme park was highly popular." He added. "Attraction for the hillbilly - themed attraction including Dibo's Water Rides, Spooky Train Ride, Volcano Roller Coaster and many more." He emphasized the word volcano. "It is also a 400 acre (1.6 square KM) abandoned theme park, which now you guys have purchased for US$ 2M (€1.5M, €1.2M) into an eco - friendly destination." We all smiled even the youngest thorn could prick, I shall say. "Also presuming the former theme park's waterfall, bridges and train, with plans to also convert one of the site's old mills into a restaurant." I mentioned. Gustin then smiled and wrapped his right arm around my waist. I smiled then did the same. It's actually true when they say love brings out the best in you. Even parts you didn't know existed. I did not mean better manners or sense of maturity. Gustin made me want to run wild, take risks and pursue my dreams with passion and integrity. Around him, I lived.

Colton voiced, "Also planning to add orchards, vineyards and a trout farm." "Yeah, we want to retain as much as the original theme park as possible" Shini said. "Not forgetting to do the green development ecotourism." Colton added. We all nodded. Gustin questioned, "Mr Lorenzo, name me the things that made this Pebble Fall Theme Park?" Mr Lorenzo answered, "It's the train, Gustin." He flipped the pages of the book and showed us the image. Gustin said, "Since the train is one of the elements that made the theme park and we have the infrastructure here, we would like to get the train back." All of us nodded. No costs or timeline for the renovation works had been set yet, though parts of the facility were expected to be on and running after 2 days. After the discussion was over, Mr Lorenzo took his leave. Colton, Jacob and Gustin would be going to the Pebble Fall Theme Park tomorrow morning since none of us had been to that park yet. They wanted to go have a look.

My gaze flickered towards Nina who seemed to be wringing her fingers. She looked lost. All of us were sitting in the living room while watching Netflix, except Gustin. Gustin had gone out to buy the phone's reload card. His phone has less credit balance. "What's wrong baby?" Colton asked. "Um... Just thinking about whatever Mr Lorenzo had said before." Nina said. Now, Jacob and Shini focused on Nina as well. She continued, "Okay guys. Since a really bad tragedy happened to the theme park years ago, don't you think that the rumours might be true." "That this mighty park is haunted", Colton smirked. Nina smacked his arm for that. "Ouch!" he exclaimed.

I uttered, "Nina darling, you don't have to worry about that. You do know that we've been facing huge deals of opposition from other companies don't you?" Jacob responded, "Keer is right. Plus, these people would do anything to see us fall. Just don't worry about it. The 3 of us would let you queens stay updated when we're headed to the park tomorrow." Nina said, "Alright. Thanks.

Kinda better now." "You better be, Nina Parrish." I exclaimed.

It was now 11 at night, but yet there was no sign of the love of my life. I tried contacting him, but the computer sound was what I heard at that point. I headed downstairs. The others were asleep. "This man's gonna get it from me when he returns." I muttered under my breath and marched towards the couch. Feeling too tired for anything, I laid on the couch and fell asleep with my poor phone by my side, just in case he called. Hours seemed to pass, then I woke up, feeling too warm, as I turned around, I felt two strong arms around me. Gustin kissed my forehead and I softly said, "You're late, honey." He whispered, "Sorry love, I had to go to Mr Lorenzo's residence and my phone died. Go back to sleep, I'm home now." I smiled and kissed his lips. "I love you." I said. We fell asleep in each other's arms.

I was awake due to the morning sunbeams shattering off my skin the next day. Not only Gustin and I were on the bed but he also had me in his arms. He must have had carried me upstairs, I thought. Gustin and I, both had never given that much of concern about our physical relationship, which means we hardly thought about losing virtue and stuffs, I shall say. He and I, fortunately, both thought that virginity was the most valuable thing that we were going to give each other after marriage. For an instant, I looked up at my sleeping Gustin who looked calm in his sleep. I loved him so much that I hoped to die in his arms, if death ever approached. With glistening eyes, I set myself up and kissed his forehead. I had to go shower then prepare breakfast.

After showering, I threw on my sleeveless purple shirt with a pair of black leggings. I let my hair drop, and sprinted downstairs. I smelled muffins. "Mm... Shini must be baking." I thought. I went into the kitchen and found Nina baking instead. She was popping big muffins out of a tin and placed them on paper plates. "Good morning, darls." Nina said. She kissed on my cheek and smiled. "Morning, hons. Smells good. I thought Shini was the one baking at first. Where are the others anyways?" I took a muffin and chewed it. It smelled wonderful like fresh blueberries. "Well, Shini and Jacob are at the backyard having some of their own time together, taking selfies." She responded. "Selfie in the backyard?" I laughed. "Alrighto." I exclaimed. "Where is Colton then?" Nina responded, "Well, you know, still sleeping." Nina and I bursted out into laugh. "I want to be making some breakfast." I uttered. I walked towards the fridge and took whatever I could make for meal. I had tortilla wheat, chocolate almond butter and ripe bananas in here. With that I opened YouTube and watched The Healthy Chocolate and Banana Quesadilla tutorial. Despite I wasn't that familiar with cooking, I had decided to try my hands out in it today. Letting out a huge breath, I followed the steps shown on the video. I first spread the almond butter over half of the tortilla, topped the almond butter with sliced bananas and folded the tortilla in in half. Next, I took the non - stick pan spray, and sprayed each other side with a quick shot. Then, in the skilled over medium - high heat, I cooked the quesadilla on each side until it into golden brown. Finally, I sliced it into halves and served it on the plate. I brought the plate close to my nose. A huge grin replaced my just now's curled lips. "I must let Gustin try this." I thought in excitement. I grabbed a tray and placed two plates of quesadilla, a carton of orange juice, with two empty glasses.

As I headed out of the kitchen, I headed towards Nina who was now talking to Colton in the living room. Shini and Jacob were there as well. "Hey guys! Have some." I said. "Oh God! Keertiga, you cooked?" Shini asked in a surprised tone yet excited. "So much of enthusiasm in me cooking?" I asked jokingly. All of them laughed, then took each one, except for Colton. He took two, and I did not worry, since I had got six quesadilla for my Gustin. "I'll have to go wake Gustin up and let him taste these, homies." I said with a huge grin walking towards the riser of the stairs. From those stares they all gave me, I could say that I must had looked like a toddler running towards the playground.

When I entered the room, Gustin was still asleep just as I had expected. The quilt was on. I set the tray aside and set myself next to him. I lowered myself towards him and stroked his hair. My face was a few inches from his. "Wake up sleepyhead." I whispered softly into his ears. Gustin opened his eyes, then smiled widely. He pulled me close to him. I kissed his lips and said, "Good morning, love." He rolled over, so that my face was under his and kissed me. He commented, "Good morning, beautiful. I smell food." He scrunched his nose. His gaze then flickered towards the tray, then he set himself up, still sitting on the bed. I handed him his plate and said proudly, "I cooked breakfast, honey. Have some." He asked, "You did? Mm... Okay." He took in a few bites of quesadilla, then his eyelids popped open wide. I was startled by that. I, being startled by his reaction, had a worried look on my face. "You don't like it, darling?" I questioned. "No, I don't like it, but I love it, sweetheart. You've just started cooking, and you're already doing great." He exclaimed. Enthusiastically, I took his face in my hands and kissed him all over the face. My lip gloss was all over his face. He had to get them washed before heading to the so called haunted Pebble Fall Theme Park with the other boys and Mr Lorenzo today.

It was now 12 noon. The boys had gone out to the theme park with Mr Lorenzo. Before leaving, Gustin promised he would let us girls stay updated on Snapchat. Even though I did see him every day, staying apart from him even for minutes hurt, I shall say. Deep inside, I actually wanted to follow, but thinking that I might seem kind off clingy, I did not.

Feeling missing, I went to the backyard to chill along with the other girls. As I set myself up the round table, my phone lit up with a few notifications on Snapchat. Gustin snapped me a few pictures of the three boys in the park. The first picture captioned THE ENTRANCE of a huge signboard with NO TRESSPASSING and VIOLATORS WILL BE PROSECUTED written on it. The board looked badly old and was surrounded by long grown weeds. As Nina and Shini looked in my direction, Nina commented, "Oh man, this place is damaged." Shini agreed, "I know right. It's been this way for like more than 2 decades." I added, Sadly vandalism and graffiti might be a serious ongoing problem for us. Plus, cleaning it up is going to be way time consuming." I furrowed my eyebrows then sighed.

I scrolled through the others pictures, then came across a few pictures of the long train ride, Dibo's Water Ride, Volcano Roller Coaster, Carousel Horse Ride, places where shows were held and so on. I then in return, took a picture of the other girls and I and sent to Gustin with caption 'SOLID'. After looking at the pictures, I could say that everything in there was real solid. Plus, as Gustin had said since we had the infrastructure there. As our first step, I shall say in our Pebble Fall Theme Park's business construction had already succeeded, all of us chilled out in the backyard having some barbecue party in the evening. We chose some of the main dishes that can be made in the cooker, marinated and grilled. We had foods like grilled skirt steak with Homemade Asian Barbecue Marinade, spicy grilled shrimp and chili - lime chicken kabobs, also not forgetting corn on the grill. Drinks were served by Shini since she had been insisting on making us drinks even when Nina and I had offered to help. "Maybe she has a new beverage to make us all." I said, raising my eyebrows. As I guessed, Shini served us all a drink which I was unfamiliar of. Its name was 'Watermelon Agua Fresca' and it tasted amazing.

I knew there was a little bit of alcohol in it, since I started feeling as if I was on cloud nine. I walked towards Gustin, who had the beverage in his hands with a goofy smile. I bumped my glass into his, and we two said, "Cheers to our first plan." We couples started dancing. I could see that Nina and Colton were a little too high. Shini and Jacob were still stable though. They seemed to be whispering something toward each other while swaying, in each other's arms. I decided to take charge as Gustin placed his hands on my hips. He and I were simply swinging our hips back giving a left about a foot between our bodies, then we started swaying our hips, arms and hands moving according to the beat. Once the dance was over, I leaned to pull him in for a kiss. We smiled in between our kiss. He leaned down to press his lips on my throat and said, "I love you."

CHAPTER 2

WELCOME, FOOLISH MORTALS

The next day, our journey to the Pebble Park Theme Park took about an hour. The view of the theme park looming up ahead made goosebumps spring up, but I could not figure out why. It was not even cold in the van. Gustin cut the engine as soon as we were at the old entrance. I could see the signboard that Gustin sent through Snapchat yesterday, vividly. It had scribbles on it. Behind the huge wall that surrounded the park, I could see the Wheel Rider and the Volcano Roller Coaster. All our gazes turned toward the sign by the main gate.

WELCOME TO THE
PEBBLE FALL THEME PARK

Most of the elements in there were abandoned. Mr. Lorenzo who had been waiting for us said "WELCOME TO PEBBLE FALL THEME PARK, girls. Since I'll be having an appointment with the doctor in a while, The boys will be showing you all around alright? "No problem, Mr. Lorenzo." Shini said. Mr. Lorenzo then left. "We have the park by our own now, don't we?'" I grinned. "Correction, Keer. It's the abandoned park." Nina emphasized the word abandoned. "Which is why I love the place." I joked with a sinister smile on my face. I placed my hand on her shoulder and soothed her. "We'll be fine, Nina Parrish."

Gustin viewed the map of the theme park in his phone, then led us to the first spot. We couples had our hands intertwined. As we walked,Gustin would occasionally kiss my hand, and I would lean in to kiss him on the cheek. After 5 minutes, of walking, Gustin said "We're now about pass by that ticket desk and explore the street." When we were near the ticket desk, I took my phone out then took a picture of the old ticket desk. Back then, visitors had to pay one for each rides. It was sort of painful to look at the mini street. The mini street was quiet and derelict.

We walked, passing by the mess of stalls that were supposed to be sell popcorns, cotton candies, burgers, and many more. The concrete of the lane was cracked and sun bleached, the stalls on each side were once gaily painted, but now peeled, crackled and flaked. The wind howled like some horror movie opener. We ignored it, regardless. "It sucks too see this place abandoned, man." Nina commented. "I know right, baby. How I wish we were alive back then so that we could come here." Colton replied "Once the park is renovated we'll have to make sure there are more options than the previous one and offer the best food and beverage service as possible." I said, handing my phone to Jacob. "Snap some pictures, Jacob. "Okie dokie." Jacob replied. "We also should sell novelty and souvenir items in order to promote our park." Gustin said. "That's a great idea, darling. We'll grab much attendance with this." I said with a bright smile on my face. The others nodded. We all headed to the next spot.

The sounds of our staggering footsteps echoed through the long weeds. There were no sounds other than our heartbeats and feet. Gustin held my hand tight. He led us to a huge tunnel. I scrunched my nose as spiderwebs brushed my face. Gustin chuckled at my expression, heaving a sigh now and then. "Relax, darling." He kissed me on the forehead. I brought his hand to my lips and kissed it. The tunnel was dark, that we had to switch our phone's flashlight on. Jacob flashed his phone, towards a few mannequins, lying at the bottom. "This is where exhibitions happened." Jacob stated. There were lots of portraits, drawing such as Picassos hung against the tunnel's wall. "Marvellous." Colton said. He took a snap of a woman's portrait which was probably giving in a right hook distance at him. Perhaps years back this tunnel was bathed in pools of yellow light. Every Picassos in there were unique. "Portraying the original masterpiece of this park can be a good way in attracting visitors. "Gustin said. We all nodded in agreement.

"Where are we headed next?" asked Nina. "To the 'Fiorella's Castle'." Colton replied. "The name's in Italy." I raised my eyebrows. "Yeah, since the previous owner was an Italian." Colton said. I was striked by the beautiness of the 'Fiorella's Castle'. It was enormous, almost Disneylandlike, except for the "Truth or Dare" signboard. We stumbled into the castle. From the horror movie posters on the walls, I could say that this place used to be the 'Ghost House'. "WELCOME, FOOLISH MORTALS." I said in a hoarse gigantic voice. I technically almost turned into an octopus seeing Colton getting startled. We all bursted into a huge crack. "Okay it's not nice to make a noise in here guys. Even a little sound echoes round like thunder." Shini said. It was kind of disappointing that most rooms in there were empty. "Let's go up this staircase." Gustin beckoned all of us to follow. My hand still in his. We went into a strange room.

My eyes darted from side to side. I did not know why I had this feeling that, we were being watched. My stomach lurched for a moment. Thinking that it was simply ridiculous, I ignored that petty thought of mine. The room had stuffs like fake fangs, wigs, costumes and old stereos. I could say that all these were used by the 'Ghost House' crew back then. That room seemed to be cut right out of the heart of the tower. A tiny slit of each side let the light in. A stone bench ran around the walls, but otherwise there was nothing much in the room. "Beautiful." I said, stunned. We all saw the whole of the Rockhurst to the east lying smiling, inspite of it looked as if it was about to rain. Gustin stood next to me and we wrapped our arms around each others waist. I leaned my head on his chest. "Yes, beautiful... You are beautiful." he said, glancing at me. I blushed for an instant and kissed him. My arms wrapped around his neck. "Do you have idea of how much do I love you?" Gustin asked, nuzzling his nose with mine. I widely smiled and said, "I love you more, anyways.". As he was about to argue, I covered his lips with mine. "I love you more than anything, darling." I said sincerely. I could feel my eyes glowing. Thanks to Colton or else I would have had forgotten the existence of the rest completely. "Can you guys see our guesthouse over there?" Colton asked. Nina exclaimed. "Yes, we ought to take a picture of this view." She snapped a picture with her phone.

After taking pictures, we headed out of the castle, ready to explore the other attraction spots. "It sucks to be walking through the spi......." I said, but stopped abrubtly. My hair was whipping so violently on my face. Strange hissing and moaning sounds began to be heard. "Gustin!!!!" I cried as I tried grabbing his hand, but his hand was out of reach. I could barely see since trendils of fog were reaching toward us. The fog entered my lungs, chilly and stiffing. My chest tightened, as though steel bands were closing around my ribs. I could barely hear nor feel anything. I gulped in more of the fog and fought to breathe. I could feel the tremor of fear in my eyes. I then drifted.

CHAPTER 3

GONE

What is life but being conscious? And good and evil are manifestations of consciousness. If you reject one, you're not getting the whole thing that's there to be had. I knew that I had been unconscious for a long time. My body was stiff, head filled with strange dreams, wild imaginings that followed one hard on heels of the next. The bad and the heavenly, all mixed together into a bizarre jumble. I struggled with it as my mind became more alert, focusing on reality. I felt the exhaustion and a sharp pang of pain on my head and body. My eyelids popped open wide. My body shivered really hard. I was drenched, not only in the rain that might had fallen when I fainted, but in pain. I tried setting myself, clothes still wet.

I was in a place I couldn't recall off. I had been lying on the carousel horse out of nowhere. Most of the horses in there were scratched and weathered, their tails broken off and their saddles chipped. It was night and monstrous howls could be heard in the abandoned park. I could feel the ghostly pale on my face. With chattering teeth, I shouted, "Gustin!" The only thing that came back tumbling was my echo. With shaky legs and streaming tears in eyes, I dashed forward as fast as I could. The rain had soaked into my shoes that I stumbled as I trudged. All I knew was I had to find Gustin and my friends. I was totally numb at that point, feeling like a lost child instead of a teenager. The tears were no help in finding my friends, to wherever I could go. My feet slipped and I was falling. I could not open my voice to scream. Fear paralysed my body. I was falling down. Down, down, down. I sobbed as I stay there, curled up on a wet bracken. I set myself up, pathetically brushing the muds off my clothes.

There was a light, unnatural breeze. My eyes flashed open. I swore I saw it darting away from the arcade games department which was at front and heading someplace inside. I trudged towards the light, ignoring the chilling blood down my spine. I was at the "Children's Playroom's door now. I was one hundred percent sure, that's where the light headed. Taking in a deep breath, I twisted the handle and welcomed myself unwillingly inside. The door creaked as I opened. Thin grey dusts flew all round then I sneezed. The playroom was dark and silent inside. There was no trace of light in. The darkness was oppressive that I did not dare to go further inside and investigate. The wind sounded its mighty roar in sudden, making everything that surrounded it shake in fear. It all happened very quickly then.

Just as I stepped my right foot out, I was being flung back. My eyes wide with horror, the scream tore through me like a great shard of glass. The door shut closed abruptly. I felt as if I've dug my own graveyard. In a heartbeat, I landed in the mess of arcade balls. I could say from the hardness. I cried, "Whoever you are, let me go!! Please!! I beg you." I could say, I was absolutely open – minded about supernatural powers that moment. I received no reply. Suddenly, I heard some strange whispers near my left ear. A bead of cool sweat dripped down my neck. I could feel there was somebody... but just ... something inhuman... I clenched my fists. I had to escape from here. Showing my fear would only make my situation worse. The whisper still went on making my legs tremble. The language was no familiar. I squeezed my eyes shut.

The whisper then turned into screaming. I screamed too and ran out of the playroom as fast as I could, unlocking the door. That was the loudest most piercing scream I had ever heard. It sounded like a scream of hysteria and disbelief, bordering on terror. As I ran I did not dare to look back, even though dozens of arcade balls were being thrown at me. The blood drained from my head as my legs pounded furiously on the uneven muddy track. I had no clue where was I heading to. I did not remember being that scared in my life. And that was just the beginning. That idea only made it worse. If that was even possible.

After reaching really far from the terrible "Children's Playroom", I stopped abruptly. I was in an amphitheatre in the theme park. I pray for God to send winds enough to cover my tracks, to wash any trace of my path and to remove my scents from wherever I had run minutes ago. I decided to take a seat at the lowest row of seat in there. The amphitheatre was circular in plan, with seating tiers that surrounded the central performance area, like an open – air stadium. I needed to breathe.

My phone was nowhere near me. I was completely empty handed and dirty. Muds all over my shoes and jeans. I walked towards the so called porticus post scaenam at front. I could see something underneath it. It laid there unmoving with pale face, I approached the solid figure.

"It's a locked box. I must open it up." I said under my breath. My eyes roamed for any key around but it was nowhere around, which made me curse under my breath. Instantly, I pulled out the hairpin off my hair and reached for the box. I remembered Gustin teaching me this once. I wasn't really good at it though.

"I can do this." I breathed. I started with bending the hairpin open until the ends were about 90 degrees apart. Next, I removed the bit of the rubber on the straight side of the pin with my teeth. I then bent the other half of the hairpin into a bit of a handle. I had to make the lever that would turn the lock now. I bent the whole bobby pin into a right angle. With shaky hands, I inserted the lever into the bottom half of the lock. Since, I wasn't sure which way would the lock turn, I tried both direction. The left was the correct one, I assumed, since the right one grinded slightly. I inserted my pick, bent in side up and felt for the pins. Fortunately, I could feel bent end pointing upwards. I pushed up specific pins with the end. I gently pushed up the pin until it made an audible "CLICK". The pin was now out of the way of the rusty lock.

Inside, there were things like costumes, bouncy balls, play dough, candles, shoe laces, hair accessories, toys and ... a baseball bat. I could say all these things were used for drama play back then. Thoughtfully, I took the baseball bat off and brushed the dusts off it. My stomach lurched.

I could feel it. I knew it was there. I felt the electric awareness seeping into my body. I took a few calming breaths. I had to run now. Someplace where I could end this stupid game.

In a heartbeat, I dashed towards the "Volcano Roller Coaster" which was now rising ahead me. The baseball bat in my left hand. I swear, I could still feel a pair of eyes attached on the back of my neck, technically.

CHAPTER 4

OUCH!!!

The roller coaster looked like a lonely skeleton. This was the only way I could find my friends. If it's not now then never, I thought. As I stared up the cross ties from the ground, my throat felt tighter. Paralyzing hurt spread through my body like icy, liquid metal. I had always been afraid of heights. But if I had to risk my life for my Gustin, Nina, Shini, Colton and Jacob, yes I would.

Holding the baseball bat in my left hand, I hesitantly took each step. My palms sweaty. Salty blood filled my mouth as I climbed. The wind was stronger now. I held on tight onto the hand rail so that I would not fall. I knew I would pass on conquering my fear of heights this way. My legs trembled as I was about to reach the peak of it.

The track was hidden above the canopy of the trees, was only sound to be heard, the sound of my own pulse throbbing in my ears. I did not dare to look down now, because I knew that I would fall down. Reality tried to tap its way into my marching brain's rhythm.

My gaze flickered around the entire theme park. I was high enough to see the skyline. My still state on the peak made my breathing become erratic, deep then shallow. My eyes looking for answers. Far from the roller coaster track the carousel and the terrible playroom looked like tunnels. The whole Rockhurst looked small. A narrow stream of moonlight filled little areas of the ground as it spotlighted, the long dark train was moving. I could still clearly see that there was a figure motionless was sitting in it.

Once again fear found me. It had told my legs to go weak and my stomach lurch. In an instant, I heard something approaching me from the left. Subconsciously I turned my head to the left, my senses were only high alert. Horror washed through my face as I witnessed a roller coaster cart approaching me, the same dreadful figure I supposed, sitting in it. It was motionless. I could not jump from this 100 feet high, or else I would die. I could not ever run, since the cart moved too fast. "3....2.....1" I jumped into the cart, ended up landing next to the motionless figure. In a heartbeat, I swayed the baseball bat in my hand and hit the figure as hard as I could. "Serves you right." I shouted. I set myself next to it, buckling my belt.

The figure then moved. It seemed to be startled as I was. It shot a panicked glance at me and cried "Ouch, Keertiga!!". "Oh My God, Nina. I'm sorry....." I apologized to Nina who was now next to me. Blood oozing from her head. The ghost wind sent our hairs whipping wildly around our eyes. "Oh My God, Keer, watch out!!!!" she screamed hysterically. There was a broken track ahead. Our eyes blazed at the end of the track as flames cool sweat beads dripping from our hairs. We surely were going to die now.

In all sudden the seats unbuckled by themselves. We were falling now, screaming with our whole body, eyes wide with horror faces gaunt and immobile. The world rushed by in a blur and I knew pain was coming. We dashed through the trees like superman but yet our expression was one of shock and horror. Instead of getting caught on one of those huge trees branches, we ended up falling into the river which was beneath the tree's twigs.

Nina and I sliced through the surface of the river, finally plunging deep into the water. With super human effort, I tried breaking the river surface, gulping for air then I was under again. We moved our arms like we were climbing rocks but it was only water around us. My limbs slowed down, stopped as we reached the buttress root of the tree. Nina was breathing heavily sitting next to me. I looked at Nina in the eye, "Oh dear, Nina." I broke down then hugged her tight. We were now temporarily safe. "Keer, the rest are all missing." Tears streaming from the corner of her eyes. "Yeah, we should find a way out of all this or we'll die." I insisted. Nina questioned, "But what are we gonna do now?" Give me a minute, Nina. I have to think." I uttered. Nina worried, studying my face with furrowed eyebrows. "Nina, do you remember being in the dark train?" I asked. Nina looked at me, puzzled. "What do you mean, Keer?" She voiced. From her facial expression, I could say that she was not joking. I said, "Well, I saw somebody in the long train, motionless when I was on the peak. And yes, the train was moving, just like the cart. Could that be... Oh God." I half - shrieked as soon as I could find my voice, shooting through two octaves. Horror washed through Nina's face. Her eyes bulging out. "We gotta go there, Keer!" Nina insisted.

Nina and I sprinted to the "Long Train Ride" as fast as we could. The "Volcano Roller Coaster" and the "Dibo's Water Ride" raced past us. Heat tore through our chest. The darkness of that night was now eerie. We stopped in tracks, seeing the train whistle blaring, the sound resonating in my chest. These things did not give me jump scares, anymore, probably because I was now used to it or maybe because I was already expecting it. Whatever the reason was, I did not know. Nina and I stood there, our sharp gazes flickering towards the moving spooky train. The train whisked through a small pitch black tunnel. We waited patiently for the train to pass by us. Our eyes focused carefully inside the train which was passing by us now. Even with the adrenaline, our feet slowed and I felt the vomit rise in my throat witnessing whatever at our sight. "Colton !!" Nina cried. Tears burst forth like water from a dam, spilling down her face. With staggering exhaustion, we approached Colton.

CHAPTER 5

KILLER

We bent our knees and piled ourselves into the train. The train glided on the rusty thin rails, its light flashing, horn blaring. Nina and I were still soaked wet. "Oh My God, baby. What happened to you?" Nina asked, horror washed through her face. I stood motionless, eyes locked at Colton's condition. Nina fell to her knees and put her head in her hands. My heart shattered seeing his face bearing congealed blood, nose smashed, his clothes were an utter mess. I wasn't joking but he looked like a fish on the sand. His face was falling one side, his speech slurred.. I could see that he was trying to say Nina's name, but his cracked lips was falling at the first syllable itself.

Nina immediately took a key out of her pocket and made Colton grip it. Colton fell into unconsciousness.

The spooky train was moving even wildly now. It was about to pass through the same tunnel. "We must jump out of this train, Nina.". I insisted. With Colton in between, Nina and I both grasped his waistband and pulled on it slightly to lift his upper body. Colton was heavy, indeed.

On three we launched off the train. Our feet slammed into the solid ground and pain prickled through my shins. The hard landing sent Colton's body sprawling on the ground. Fear thoughts looped around my mind as Nina and I lifted Colton until there was no room for anything else. Tears streaming down my check as we stumbled. I wondered in which state would Gustin be at now. I was lost in time, blinded by the tears in my eyes, while the pain continued to abuse me. I could not picture anybody hurting him. Terrified as I was, I felt myself sinking down into depression, drowning in it.

The wind screamed more than howls. Torrential pored down in icy sheets like needles upon our faces. The trees and weeds bent and moaned in wrath enough to scare the Gods, branches torn like paper limbs. Nina and I, with Colton sprinted to a small cave which had "The Mini Jungle" sign on it. This is where they used to hold wild animals exhibition like snakes, parrots, and alligators.

We stayed in the cave, my gazes flickering carefully outside it. Attacks might approach any times towards us. We had to get ourselves prepared in any case. Nina had her legs crossed. Colton's head laying on her lap. Tears began to spill from her helpless eyes onto Colton's cheek. I knew how she felt at the moment, every bit of it. I looked away from Nina and continued gazing at the soil ahead of the cave. I was grieving. When the evil supernatural creature could take a huge toll on Colton, why wouldn't it do that to my Gus...., I paused thinking. That thought simply stood there with bloody short red eyes, embracing the emptiness in my heart and a shear of nothingness. Something was poking above the soil. I could see that. The heavy rain was trying to reveal something. "Nina!!Nina!!Come here!!" I shouted. She ran towards me, hastily and asked "What is it??" I pointed my left index finger towards the soil. It became even vivid now. I smelled something which made me feel sick, even in this heavy downpour. "Mr. Lo..Lo...Lore....nzo" Nina stuttered. I pressed my palm to my lips and screamed as I reached towards Mr. Lorenzo. He laid there on his back, lifeless. His black eyes were wide open, but his jade irises held an uncontrollable grief. His coat and suit were bloody. My eyes burnt and I was too weak to rise. The sight of blood made me sick. I wanted to rest my head on the wet ground and let that be the end of it.

CHAPTER 6

EPIPHANY

My heart pounded as one question continued to race through my mind, "What does the thing want from us?" Nina and I both gently lifted Mr. Lorenzo's body and placed him in the cave. I brought my palms to his eyes and closed them carefully. Nina picked a dandelion flower growing in there and placed it on his motionless chest, between his folded arms. "Rest In Peace, Mr. Lorenzo" I said under my breath.

The storm had now stopped. We stumbled from "The Mini Jungle" cave, Colton still unconscious. Finding Mr. Lorenzo's dead body and placing him in the cave was still running across my mind, like a boomerang, I shall say. I had never encountered a corpse in my life before. After whatever had happened to us in the Pebble Fall Theme Park, I felt as if the impact had knocked every wisp of air from my lungs. That was how I felt now, totally speechless and struggling to breath.

"Nina Parrish." I called her full name. She glanced up from her eyes lids catching my eyes. "What is it, hons?", she asked. "I think I'm having an epiphany here.. "I said. She waited for me to speak.

I thought about everything which happened to us all while we were in this theme park. Being chased was not at all like the movies. All these adrenalines, blood, death and chase had to stop. I was literally sick of them all. I decided to put a full stop on this stupid hide and seek game. One wrong move and we all would die. No second lives. I shuddered at that thought.

"Nina, the best way to run away from a problem is to face it. We need to communicate with 'the thing'." I said. Nina looked at me in disbelief as I had expected. "No, you're insane. Do you know how dang....." Nina stopped halfway since I interrupted her. "For how long is this gonna go, Nina? This is the only chance we have. Stay strong." I sternly said. I grabbed her left shoulder and gave a peck on her forehead. I knew this would be risky. But if it worked, I couldn't be more relieved.

Nina and I, Colton, aside sat across-legged on the ground. We were circled by the Ferris Wheel, Bumper car, and Swing Rides. Surprisingly neither the trees nor the weeds dared to rustle as if they were tensed with nerves for what was to come. "Nina, just follow whatever I do, alright? Victory is ours." I said. Nina nodded, even though she wasn't really alright with us communicating with the supernatural. Before we began, I took my chain off my neck. I told myself constantly, "This is going to be worth it. "I didn't really like removing the chain, since it was Gustin's birthday gift for me. For him, I had to do this. I held the chain straight with my dominant hand. Nina had her hand on mine.

"Is anybody here with us?" I asked. Nina glanced around. "The chain started swaying in a circular motion. My breath came in small spurts, hot and nervous. Nina looked as if she was about to faint any moment. Her grip on my hand tightened.

"Dear spirit, we demand to know about your unsettled debt towards us". The chain started swinging again. Nina's face stayed ghostly pale. It was keeping on swinging and it was faster now. I was really on my nerves now.

"Dear spirit, I demand you to reveal yourself." The chain swung faster and faster. I felt something blew on my bare neck. Tension grew in my face and limbs, my mind replaying the last attack. The swinging chain then flee off my grip. My eyes widened in horror, gaze flickering to Nina. But Nina seemed to be looking somewhere else... some place near me. Her body shaking really hard.

"Keer.. it is... loo..looking right at you" she gasped, her eyes glassy.

"Ohhh Myyy Goddd!!!! It is right next to you." She cried in horror. I froze. At first it was a deep moaning sweeping over my left ear. The sound wounded itself around my ear and began to change, like a terrible lullaby. I started to sweat, my heart beating faster. It was no language I knew, but it hissed as it spoke. I could feel pair of eyes glaring at me. Its stinky breath on my neck.

I turned my head to the left slowly. Body still shaking. Here it was. It was a woman. The emaciated woman had dirt and grit all over her clothes and grimy body. Her face was pale, her jaw showing her torn tongue and blood-stained, razor sharp, savage teeth. There was a hurricane inside me. My sweat dripping as the creature turned its head slowly towards Nina. It happened too fast then.

Nina was being flung back that her back hit the stem of the tree nearby. She let out a piercing scream. Her dead weight was too was almost too much to prevent the momentum taking her to the ground. I watched in horror. The figure's red eyes flickered towards me. I felt an invisible hand clasping over my mouth. A flame of anger seemed to ignite within that 'thing'. It let out a piercing screech and charged towards me. The scream squeaked through by scorched throat. It was a hysterical scream. I witnessed the stars watching from the heavens. Its horrid face looming over mine. Salty tears clouded my eyes. My vision clouded, the world and my Gustin faded away. Blackness.

CHAPTER 7

DRAINED...

My head was a carousel of fears spinning out of control, each one pushing my mind out of blackness. I heard sounds not far away from the place I lied. I opened my eyes in a place of incredible joy. Instead of waking up in a place full of grown weeds as I expected, I woke in a place filled with laughter. I gazed around, I was sitting on the ground where I had been lying on, my mind dazed. I was 100% sure that I was not dreaming. It took time for me to absorb the surrounding as I looked around. I was in the same theme park. But... everything in here was different now. It was a grand theme park.

There were pale faced kids running around, a few teenagers and adults riding on the Bumper Car, some being swung on the Swing Ride, while some on the Ferris Wheel. Everything seemed different. I stood there dazed. I could not bring myself to senses. Stumbling, I reached towards Nina who was unconscious under the tree. "Darls, wake up!! Everything around us has changed!! Nina wake up." I cried. In seconds, her eyelids popped open wide. She was startled.

Subconsciously, she brought her palm to the back of her head. "Ouch!" She claimed. Her gaze flickered to my deadly pale face then towards our surrounding. I could say she was about to scream as her breath came out in gasp. I knew her too well. I instantly pressed my palm against her mouth. I lowered my head then whispered cautiously, "Shh...Nina. We need to walk away from here. We have to pretend as if we don't see them." I stuttered. My heart felt as it was going to explode in the inside. "Nina, I don't feel this people are inhuman." I shuddered at the word inhuman. Cool sweat dripping from my forehead. "We'll have to pretend as if we don't see them, darls. Running away will only make them chase us." I said, fighting my struggle to breathe.

Nina instantly nodded. Fear written all over her face. I took my palm off her mouth. Her lips trembled. "We've faced lots in this stupid theme park, Nina. Keep yourself strong. I don't know what's happening here but moving forward seems to be the only way we have." I, myself was not brave enough but I could see that Nina needed more help.

Nina and I scooped Colton in our arms and trudged towards the souls ahead of us. With the corner of my eyes, I could see that those spirits were in the 60's outfits, like the trouser suits and box – shaped dresses. My stomach did its usual routine again. I was completely aware that these spirits had their black eyes on us. Every spirits stayed in groups in every of the theme park's department. I knew I might had looked like a warrior from the outside, but inside I was so against my throbbing heart. "Put on a show, Keertiga. Show your fear, you're dead." I told myself. Nina had her eyes on the ground. Her face had a dead expression. My eyes forward. I swore I saw teenage spirits flying with popcorns in their hands. I pretended as if I saw nothing though.

I was then startled by a huge hand clamping over my mouth, an equally ghostly hypodermic of adrenaline pieces my heart, unloading in an instant. Subconsciously, my grip in Colton faded. I couldn't scream. Nina screamed. The souls around us screamed as well. Their bodies seemed to fly away. Their faces changed to an ugly ghostly, frightening sight and passed through our bodies like radioactive rays. The theme park changed to its actual forgotten state back. The huge hand was still pressed on my mouth. The souls then disappeared into thin air.

In an instant, I was being scooped up lightly to the collarbone in a familiar way... really familiar. I looked up with questioning eyes, "Gustin!!" Nina exclaimed. Her jaw dropped. I was sure it was not some kind of hallucination. Here I was, in his arms. It was really him. My heart dropped seeing his condition. He was more purple than white. His left eye was swollen. His face bore congealed blood and clothes were an utter mess. There were circles under his eyes. His glistening eyes burnt into mine. My throat felt heavy. Tears trickled out of my eyes and I could not stop them.

In a heartbeat, Gustin pulled me in and hugged me tight. My chin resting on his shoulder. My arms wrapped around his back. "Darling! It's okay. I'm back now. We'll get through this together, alright?" He croaked. I could say he was about to cry as well. I pulled back a little and held his wounded face and did circles on his cheeks with my thumbs. "Look at what has the thing done to you, love." I was sobbing even harder now. I kissed all over his face and hugged him really tight. He rubbed my back continuously. "It's okay, love. Let it all out. I love you." he said. With the crying face, I held his face and pressed my sore lips against his. I leaned my forehead against his. "We need to get out of here, girls. Nina, leave Colton to me." He said. "But honey, what about Shini and Jacob then?" I asked. "They're...they're dead." He stuttered. His eyes burnt towards the trees ahead telling an unknown story. I pressed my palm hard on my mouth and screamed. Nina fell to her knees. "Why is this happening to us?" I sobbed, hugging Gustin really tight. His already ruined clothes was now messed with my tears. Shini and Jacob were dead? I could not keep myself upright. Emotionally we're done, mentally we're drained and spiritually we're dead. Tonight the sky was utterly black just as our states. It had been black for for a really long time now. I shivered, though it wasn't cold. I looked up to the watching skies. We had lost our best friends, Shini and Jacob. I also knew really well that we were being watched and we would not be spared too.

CHAPTER 8

MAZE

Jacob had been the most overprotective of us all. Even when Nina and Colton had any arguments, he would actually talk to Colton even when it was actually Nina's fault. He was like a big brother to us all. As for Shini, she was a great sister to Nina and I. I had always adored her ability in cooking and staying calm in difficult situations. Nina and I cried like a "kid noisily, with running snot and choking sobs clumsily. Gustin held me in his arms, never releasing his grip on me. He was brushing my hair back and forth. I could see the conflict in him already, him wanting to be strong for me and the raw need to weep welling up. "Let it all out, Gus." I croaked.

That was all the permission my Gus needed, head down on my shoulder, his arms wrapped around me even tighter. He was crying really hard now. "My Gus..." I croaked, my lips against his hair. He and I needed to stand up for each other now.

Gustin pulled out from our long hug then lifted Colton. I could not help but be amazed on how swift Gus lifted him. He motioned us to follow him. His dark eyes puffy. We all accelerated towards, the entrance. Getting out of this stupid theme park was the only craving we had.

The view of the entrance looming up ahead, made my breathing became even rapid. The wind blew erratically against our skills as we were driving on highways with the windows down. Our hairs became like a flag, and the noise of crashing objects screamed more than howls. Subconsciously I squeezed my eyes shut to keep out the violent dust. I could, but yet barely, see the entrance gates opening then close repetitively as if it was making fun of us.

Abruptly, we bent down and pressed ourselves to the ground, arms on each other. Gustin had Colton pinned under him. They would have looked like gays if we weren't in a complex situation like this.

I stopped in tracks. I knew I was not dreaming again. Nina had the same facial expression as mine. Gustin already had his eyes on me. His jaw tensed. I let out a huge breath seeing whatever ahead of us this time. We were in a maze. In current's case, we were as if in Alice In Wonderland now. Every hedges were tall and a uniform green. "O-H- M-Y-G-O-D." Nina shuddered. "We're trapped." I added.

My eyes flickered towards Gustin. He stared deadly forward and said "Don't just gaze, change your pace......to win the race". His gaze flickered towards confused Nina and I. "What??"Nina furrowed her eyebrows. "There has to be a way." Gustin gasped. In a heartbeat, I heard a dreadful hysterical laugh behind us. I was sure Gustin and Nina heard it as well. Fear covered chill spiked the tip of my tongue. "Ignore it. Don't turn behind." he said. Nina stood motionless. Gustin had his palm circled around my wrist. The sound ripping away at my ear drums with its repetitive noise, increasing by the second.

In a heartbeat, we blasted to whatever space ahead of us, never daring to ever glance behind. We accelerated in an attempt to find a way out, my eyes following the space ahead. Gustin was a warrior indeed, He had Colton on his right shoulder while on the other hand, he enclosed my wrist tighter. We kept on stumbling for what seemed minutes now. We had come across lots of dead ends now. All around us were just tall hedges, whatever ahead of us only led us to the wrong way. There were so many dark hours ahead and my feet felt sore.

We abruptly stopped someplace in the maze and fell into our knees. I was really thirsty now. Nina brought her palms to the face and startled crying. For some reason, I started sobbing as well. All these were just too much for me to take in. I immediately reached towards Gustin who was sitting next to me. He had already laid Colton on the ground aside by then.

I brought his hand to my forehead and sobbed. He pulled me in and held me really tight. He started crying as well now. His eyes were bloody shot red. My head buried in his collarbone. "We've got only two choices for now, darling." Gustin croaked. I nodded, tears still welling up on my cheeks. I leaned my forehead against his. "It's either walk the maze by night or slip into hypothermia." he added. His eyes burnt into mine. He held my face with his hands and pressed his lips against mine. I kissed him back hungrily. There was something different about our kiss. Our lips became very much demanding. The kiss had some painful edge for some reason I couldn't imagine.... Losing each other. Gustin pulled back and said seriously, "I'm not letting anything happen to you, love. No matter.... what...what happens to me you'll.." I silenced him by covering his lips with mine. "Never say that again, you idiotic moron. I've always wanted to die in your arms if death ever approaches." I croaked. I had already lost my unbiological siblings and I did not want to lose the love of my life now. I hugged Gus even tighter, wishing I could marry him right away. The most painful goodbye were the ones that were never said and never explained.

CHAPTER 9

I L.O.V.E. YOUR SUFFERING

"OH MY GOD, guys come here!!" Gus and I were startled by Nina's shrieking. "What is it?" We rushed towards Nina, our eyebrows furrowed. "Co...Colton's moving." She said. Hope written all over her face. The tension that had kept her up for hours of night melted into nothing.

We all surrounded Colton. One click and his eyes slowly opened. "Baby!!" Nina exclaimed. She placed her both palms on his cheeks. Colton tried smiling. His gazed then flickered towards mine. Tears started clouding his vision. "Colton, you're alright?" I asked. "Shini and Jacob are dead, Colton. Mr Lorenzo's dead as well. We're trapped in a bloody maze now." I croaked. I was about to cry too now. Unexpectedly as he diverted his gaze towards Gustin, horror seemed to wash through his face. His eyes were wide. Sweat dripping down his forehead. A small gasp left his lips. He was draining now. "COLTON!" Nina cried. He pointed his finger towards Gustin. I could say his lips failed at first syllable of Gustin's name itself. His lips cracked. I turned my head slowly and looked at Gus. His face was motionless and expressionless as he looked at Colton. I held Colton's face in my hands and urged, "Colton, what is it?? What is that you want to tell us?" It happened too fast then.

Nina, Gus and I witnessed what looked like a dragging right before our very eyes. Colton was suddenly dragged by something invisible along the maze. His eyes were bulging. Every muscles in my body knotted up we all ran towards Colton, trying to get a grip on his leg. I was seriously terror - stricken. Gustin had a grip on his leg but then it slipped. What was really horrible to see that he disappeared through hedges. "OH. MY. GOD," Nina shrieked, her voice itself frightened me. "COLTON!!!" I called out loud and tried running my hands through the hedges but couldn't. Nina fell onto her knees, she looked as if she was trying to absorb whatever had been happening. There was utter silence for a moment. Neither of us talked. None of us knew what to do.

Then, something gave in a right look distance at me. I examined the hedge where Colton was being dragged. Suddenly, I felt something rusty dripping down my forehead. I touched my forehead then examined my forehead. "BLOOD!!!"

"ARGHHH!!" I screamed. Gus and Nina rushed towards me. "What is it, darling??" He wrapped his arms protectively around me. I pointed my finger to the ground. Like millions of red flowers blooming, the droplets of blood fell onto the ground and created a word. I was pretty sure those blood were not from my forehead. Those bloods formed "TRAITOR".

"TRAITOR?" Nina questioned. I saw Gustin mumbling incoherently under his breath. His arms were still around me. "I'm having an epiphany here." "What is it, love?" I asked. Nina and I paid close attention. "I feel this word in here is a getaway." He said. "A getaway to?" Nina asked. "To be revealing the hidden truth." Gustin voiced. I stared into his eyes, with the strucked realisation. I looked back on the ground. My eyebrows furrowed. "TRAITOR."

CHAPTER 10

DARK SECRET LOVE..

"Guys....... Look over there." I pointed to the ground shakily. There was a blood trail formed along the maze. The word 'TRAITOR' was the beginning point. Yet even though the was a path, I knew none would follow it. "Guys, lets not move ahead." Nina insisted. "'This seems like anoth....'" Before she could finish her sentence, Gustin interrupted. "No, Nina. This is it !! The getaway to the curse or truth or so whatever." he claimed. Nina and I had our arms crossed as we stared at Gustin in disbelief.

"Yes, it is a getaway.... to another bloody trap." Nina said. She was losing it now. "Wait..Nina..I think Gus has a point. Who knows, we might be able to get out of this mess after revealling the hidden truth or curse so whatever." I explained. "I'm doing this, because this is our only hope Keer." Nina said. I nodded with glistening eyes. We might have a slim chance, a reason to hope and struggle onward.

Gustin had a grip on my right hand as he motioned us to follow him. I staggered back at the sight of the red liquid along the maze. The colour swirled in my mind making me feel light headed while curiousity rose in my head. Our eyes followed the path, forcefully.

We turned left, walked straight up, turned right, walked and walked until at some point where I felt faintly nauseated. I stopped in my tracks. My eyes were squeezed shut.

As I opened my eyes, I found myself standing under the Ferris Wheel perhaps. I could barely see since my vision was clouded. I wasn't in the maze anymore and I was all alone. My heart hammered inside my chest. I saw something ahead of me... something really bad. There was a dark figure. Not sure, there was one or two. Even in that clouded vision, I could see a few images running like a slideshow ahead of me. All I managed to catch up was an image of a bloody knife and yes, somebody was being killed ahead of me.

In all sudden, the dark figure started to approach me. Neither Gustin nor Nina were around me. My limbs screamed to run but I just couldn't. My breaths come in gasps and I felt like I would black out. The entire theme park spun and I fell onto my knees, trying to make everything slow. I felt so sick. I squeezed my eyes shut, praying. "Keertiga!! Keertiga!! Darling!! Love!! Are you alright??"

My eyelids popped open wide I was panting desperately. "Darling, are you alright? Gustin asked impatiently. His arms shook my body hard that my teeth rattled a little. I was still in the maze but yes, on my kness. Desperately, I reached up for Gustin and hugged him tight as I cried. He wrapped his arms tightly around me and he constantly brushed my hair." Honey, calm down..." Tell us what was it."" Gustin said softly.

I pulled back and croaked, "I saw... I found myself under the Ferris Wheel just now. Something tragic was happening, Gus. The thing was trying to kill me." I sobbed. Nina pressed her palm to her lips and cried. Gus pulled me in his arms and croaked in tears, "I'm not letting anything harm you, my love." He kissed my forehead. "But what if... what if it has something to do with the truth." he said. Nina and I paid close attention to Gus.

"Honey, what else did you see? "he asked, staring deep into my pupils. "There was this...sight of blood as well." I shuddered. "These were the only things I witnessed so for." I said. "Oh!! Wait, wait." I said. "There was something else. Before the thing tried killing me, it was actually getting rid of somebody else. I couldn't really see who that person was." My lips trembled.

***THREE THINGS CANNOT BE LONG HIDDEN,THE SUN,THE MOON AND THE TRUTH.-CONFUCIOUS.

CHAPTER 11

GREAT LOSS

"Love, breath okay. As long as I'm with you, no two faced demons can hurt you." His jaw tensed. I threw my arms around him, sobbing as I tried absorbing his words. "It's just hard to fight when the fight isn't fair, my love." I croaked. He held my face and drew circles on my cheeks as he said, "It was never from your foes, Keertiga Chandran." "Wait, what??" Nina asked. Our gazes flickered towards Nina who was standing ahead us. But something else captured my attention. I stood like a bird locked in the gaze of snake. My eyes had that wide look.

"Shini...Jac..." my voice came out thin. There they were, pale faced standing few steps behind Nina. It all happened too fast then. The ground behind

Nina began cracking apart. Nina screamed. Nina was falling now. With the adrenaline rush, Gustin and I ran to Nina but only Gustin was the one managing to reach her first. "Nina, give me your hand!" Gustin said. My body shivered from the very intense wind. Nina was hanging from the ground, by her hand. Below her, there was a huge fireplace that looked like hell for eternal damnation. Cold crept up my spine. I reached my hand for Nina. "Nina, bring your right hand up!" I shouted. The wind blew harder. Really hard that I had to lean against Gustin to stay on feet or else I will fall in as well. I looked down in despair, my end was coming. All at once, my foot slipped down and the scenery to blur like a poorly shot action photograph. Nina screamed. The three of us were falling into the hell of eternal damnation now. The hot blazing flames reached out for us, its hands wrapped around us, pulling us down. We screamed as the flame gulped us down. The expected burning into ashes did come and instead we were still falling, only now it was utterly black.

After a few seconds... THUMP! My eyes squeezed as my face contorted. Everything hurt now, my back especially. I tried standing, trying to comprehend what was going on around me and where I was. I looked around. I was in a familiar place now. I was under the Ferris Wheel again, alone. I immediately knew that I wasn't apparently there. My body was someplace else. I clenched my teeth together. "I have to do this." I thought.

I slowly turned my head forward. Everything was clear and vivid now. Probably if I had faced this one, everything that had been happening to us would come to an end. As I expected there were two dark figures trying to murder...

My breath stopped... "Gus..." A small gasp escaped my mouth. I ran towards the two hooded figures, trying to reach for them. Unfortunately, my hands only passed through one of the figures like a radioactive ray. Horror washed through my face.

I shouted, "STOP! Leave him alone!" None of them seemed to see nor hear me unfortunately. I was 100% sure that I wasn't dead since I had the same experience minutes ago. It was vivid this time. Tears gushed down my cheek. I was pleading now.

"YOU TRAITOR!" Gustin's jaw clenched. He gave the tall figure a hard punch on the face that he fell. The hood went down. My eyes went wide. I stood there struggling to inhale, to exhale, to do anything. I was pale now. "J...Ja...Jake...JACOB..." I stuttered. My gaze flickered towards the other figure. It was Sh...SHINI... My heart fell. I was all numb now. Shini walked towards Gustin and gave him a tight slap that it echoed in the theme park. "You and Jacob were like brother and sister to us! We trusted you, moron! And this is how you repay us! This?! Sending evil spirits to kill us down! Playing this stupid hide and seek game!Killing Mr.Lorenzo! Wanting all of my property! Taking over this business to all yourselves! You better stop before I rip your throat out. You know if Keer was here, how heartbroken she would be? She would chop your heads off you little pieces of illegitimate s**t!" Gus screamed. Tears gushing down his cheeks. My limbs were weak. We were betrayed.

With devilish smirk, Shini sat the knife precariously on his skin, soft enough not to pierce his neck, hard enough to enforce the intended message.

I stood there and watched, being helpless and cornered, praying.

"Jake honey, I guess we should tell him the Man and The Snake's' story before ending his life." Shini smirked. Jacob slammed his lips to Shini's, his tongue fighting against hers. I looked away. I was disgusted not because of the kiss but because of the betrayal these two had done to us.

"Well, Gustin Collins, about the man and snake, in...in pity, he brought the poor snake." Shini said. Gus gave Shini a punch on the nose and made her cringe. The knife slipped out of her hand. In a heartbeat, Jacob caught the knife and stabbed Gustin's stomach. "Noooooooooo.....!!" My throat tore. Those traitors laughed mercilessly.

"Aww! Let me finish, Gus. In pity he brought the poor snake,To be warmed at his fire. A mistake! For the ungrateful thing. Wife & children would sting." My Gus's skin was tearing to shreds as the knife rotated, the sound of his muscles and nerves being gouged louder. I saw it all. I cried as if the ferocity of it might save the love of my life. I hated myself for it. He was my baby, my soulmate and he should not die. "Don't kill him. Let my Gus go!

Let my baby go! He's innocent!" I screamed at the very top of my lungs. *"Avena vidu!Aven paavam daa! Enna paavam senjom unggalakku! Enggala vidu Naangga porom*! Can't see him enduring too much of pain!" I first pleaded in Tamil. My Gus sank to his knees, continuing to scream, convulsing and trembling, blood flowing from the gaping hole in his back. I fell onto my knees as well, inches away from my Gus. "Darling, breathe please... Stay... I love you, baby! I can't live without you. You're my world." I pleaded.

His blue eyes bloody shot red. His breath came in ragged, shallow gasps. I watched my baby suffer. Those traitors turned away as his plead for mercy became quieter. God himself was my enemy now. He slowly got laid on the ground. There was no movement now. His heartbeats were getting slower and slower. I sat there with dead expression on my face, like a child who had lost her mother. He struggled as he said for the very last time, "You slashed at me with betrayal, I'll parry with my vengeance. I'll protect... what's mine. I... I... love you, Keertiga Chandran." That was his last breath. His heartbeat stopped. That's when mine technically stopped. "Our hearts beat together, Gus." I said with a dead expression on my face. The whole world had vanished now. My mouth was open, an eternal silenced scream, saliva dripping from behind of my teeth and onto the ground, stained with the memory of him I've ever loved.

~**TRANSLATION: *"Avena vidu! Aven paavam daa! Enna paavam senjom unggalakku! Enggala vidu Naangga porom!"*

"Leave him! He's innocent! What sin have we ever committed towards you!Leave us! We'll go away!"

CHAPTER 12

OVERWORLD IN FLAMES

"Keertiga!! What's happening? What do you see now?" I heard Nina's voice echoing. But, I had to witness more. I had to focus. "Not yet, Nina!!" I said firmly, gritting my teeth. I knew she heard me well. I had stay in this vision.

"We need to hide him someplace. Should we bury him near Lorenzo's or will that take time? Shini asked without even a percent of humanity. "We'll just hide him here someplace." We can't let the rest go, remember." He replied disgustingly. Those betrayers then lifted my Gustin's motionless body then walked towards a small control room behind the Ferris Wheel. I followed their steps unsteadily. I watched them unblock the ornate metal fastening, lift the lid then place my world in the old oak chest.

Tears streamed down my cheeks, and I screamed at the very top of my lungs. I couldn't even touch anything in here. None of these traitors heard me. The lid shut was lowered. "Darling, wake up!! Please!!" I sobbed. Realization hit hard through me. It was Gustin's spirit which was with Nina and I in the maze. He knew it all, and that's the why he was giving riddles. My upper body and shoulders wracked with every sobs that forced their way out.

"Keer!! Keer!! Come back!!" Nina's voice echoed. I wide opened my eyes. Nina had her arms wrapped around me. I found ourselves standing at the carousel department. "Nina....., where is Gustin? I asked shakily. "Keer, I'm sorry. We were falling down from the maze then ended up here. But he alone is....?" I let her words trait as my long legs carried me, bolting down the theme park. The pounding noise of my shoes resonated with a loud echo that matched my throbbing heart inside. Nina ran along, her mind completely clueless.

The view of the Ferris Wheel looming up ahead took its huge toll in my adrenaline. "Keertiga!! Wait!! Where are you going?" Nina shouted. I made my pace into control room. There was on old oak chest with some dried blood stains on it. Nina stopped in her tracks and stood next to me. With shaky hands, I unbuckled the metal fastening and lifted the lid.

A moment of silence, then Nina screamed hysterically.

The love of my life was in, just like I had seen in the vision.

Those greenish eyes which that I loved to stare at staring. The face that I adored was pale. The lips that kissed me were bluish. The stomach that I loved wrapping my hands around from the back had been stabbed. The arms that held me tight when I was sad or lost laid unmoving. Nina lifted my soulmate's body and placed it on the floor. I sank down onto his side, stewing at his face. Nina kneeled next to me as she wept. I lowered myself as I laid my head on his unmoving chest, feeling for a pulse of heartbeat. None.

My tears splashed onto his shirt as I laid there with him. My warm arms wrapped around his cold neck. "Darling...come back to me... like when we were in the maze. Would you still have been with me if I did not discover the truth? Come back to me baby, please. I love you. Who else do I have?" I cried as if that the ferocity could bring my Gustin back. He was my love. The only love of my life and he shouldn't be gone. Nina tried holding me back, to calm but in my hysteria I was too strong, too wild.

I raised my head slowly then kept my legs crossed, holding the love of my life in my arms. I startled singing, rocking back and forth. "'Your arms are my castle....[cries].... Your heart is my sky... They wipe away tears that I cry....Oh the good and the bad times we've been through them all... You make me rise when I fall...[tears escaped from the eyes].. Cuz every time we touch I get this feeling and every time we kiss I swear I could fly...Can't you feel my heartbeat fast. I want this to last...Want you in my life...." I cried hysterically hugging him. I brought my lips to his cold forehead that my tears ran to his eyes. I brought my palm to his eyes and closed them. "Shini and Jacob... I promise. I'll be hurting you so bad" my jaw clenched. "What? What are you saying, Keer?" Nina asked. " Those traitors are the reasons for our entire problem in the theme park. I've seen that in the vision." I gritted my teeth. Nina pressed her palm to her mouth and cried.

My need for revenge was like a blazing flame. The flame burnt hot short and violent. I would bare a grudge until I died or took revenge, whichever come first. Settling old sores. Brutal. Excessive. Mean spirited. For my Gustin, yes, I had to do this. Injustice had been done towards all of us, towards my baby especially.

"What else did...." Nina stopped halfway as a familiar voice was heard behind us. "Well, well. Congratulations. You two have made it till here." Shini fakely exclaimed. I glared, Shini and Jacob were in the control room now.

CHAPTER 13

MIKE TYSON

"The chase is over now." Jacob said in an evident delight. Nina flickered a glance at me. Her glossy eyes then turned furiously towards Shini and Jacob. "You!! Traitors!!" She launched at Shini. In a heartbeat, before I could react, Jacob slammed Nina hardly against the floor. Pain was written all over her face, while I stared in horror.

"Don't!!" I screamed, running forward. Jacob brought his fist to my face, snapping my nose. I cried in pain. Jacob threw his arms around me in an unbreakable grasp and dragged me out. "Leave me!!" I shouted. Nina was being dragged by Shini. It is better to die fighting then to die giving up." I thought. We were now at the similar place, where my Gustin was killed, near the Ferris Wheel.

We were then pushed to the ground. "OUCH!" I cried. Suddenly, I felt a cool breath on my neck. Then suddenly movement, so much force in every blow. I rained blows a Jacob as if I meant to smash him into the very earth. I was surprised at my own actions from outside as if...somebody else was in my body. I could feel Nina and Shini watching me in fear. Jacob was thrown back. He fell onto the ground. Pain was written all over his face. I found myself walking towards Shini now. My eyes blazed with rage. The unmoving gaze was accompanied by deliberate slow breathing. As I mentioned, I felt as if I was watching myself. Shini gulped nervously.

I gave her a tight slap, probably causing her head to reel sickeningly as she fell to the ground. She looked at me in fear, eyes watering. I was astounded myself. I walked towards Jacob now. He pleaded. "NO!! NO KEER! LEAVE US ALONE! JUST LET ME GO!" Cold sweats dripped from his forehead. I wrapped my hand around his throat and lifted him up, my thumb wedged under his chin. My eyes said nothing. I was clearly... possessed.

He fell as I released. He gasped for oxygen. "Keertiga! WATCH OUT!" Nina screamed. Just in time, I turned and kicked her abdomen. The baseball bat fell along with her. It was a sudden defence. She was a backstabber, obviously.

I grabbed the baseball bat and hit her head forcefully. Blood gushed down her forehead. She fell into unconsciousness. Nina screamed, "Keer! No! Don't! It will be a CRIME then. You will be caught by the cops then. Leave them. We'll just hand them over to the police. You've beaten them enough, sweetheart."

I could sense I was no longer a sweetheart. This simply wasn't me. I was controlled by something else. I swayed the baseball bat higher and beat Jacob Watson as I wanted him to be smashed that there would nothing left of him to be buried. He fell to the ground, sprawled now. These two would probably survive till tomorrow.

I found myself falling onto my knees as I squeezed my eyes shut and prayed for whatever was possessing me to go out. Tears ran down from the corner of my eyes. I opened my eyes as I felt the similar cold breeze on the neck. There he was.

The love of my life, Gustin Collins standing next to me. His face giving me a warm smile as always, except for the fact that his skin looked powdery, like chalk. I stood up. Nina had her tears in her eyes. I pressed my forehead into his collarbone. Tears gushed down uncontrollably on my cheek. "Life has been really unfair towards the two of us, my love." I sobbed. He brushed my hair as he held me. I shrieked as I sobbed. That was the worst kind of cry. I did not want to let him go. I knew this was a temporary reunion but yet it felt home.

CHAPTER 14

TEMPORARY REUNION

"Darling, look at me ...." he softly said. I looked at him slowly with bloody shot red eyes, still sobbing. "Love....." he held my face with both of his hands. "Gustin.... Stay please, honey. Stay... please ... Don't leave." I sobbed. He gave me a soft smile. Inspite of that, his eyes were glassy. He kissed my forehead then said, "No love, I can't. My love, first of all, I just want you to know how very much I love you. My love, leaving you is the hardest thing I'll ever have to do. You are so very special to me, sweetheart. I see you as a gift from God. The best day of my life was the day you said I love you too for the very first time. Every time I saw you smile, my heart would just melt. My life wasn't complete until I met you, my love. In minutes I may not be here right now, but take comfort in the fact that I will be watching over you. I'll not be gone and I'll always be with you in spirit. Every time you feel this cold breeze on your neck, it's just me by your side, honey. I know this must be difficult for you but my baby is strong, isn't she? God knows what's the best, honey. I love you."

"No!!!" I screamed as I fell onto my knees holding his feet, I'm pleading to you honey. Don't leave me. How am I going to live without you? [cries] Who else do I have for me? [screams] '' He immediately held my shoulders then lifted me up. He pulled me into his arms and held me tight. His usual cologne scent was still there. "*Yen maa enna vittu poringgeh? Yennaku yaaru maa irukkaa?*" I expressed in Tamil. My legs were shaky. This pain was simply unbearable.

"My dear, I'll protect you wherever you go. If you ever need me, just close your eyes and pray a moment and I'll be there'' he said. "It's time for me to go now. ''he added. I was breathless now.

For the very last moment, he held my face, drawing his mouth to mine. His hands sliding up to knot in my hair. I had to give the best out of me since this was the only reunion we could get. Everything was quiet. There was only the taste of his tongue and the swell of his lower lip. Tears streamed from the corner of our eyes as we kissed. I tried to show him in the kiss on how much would I miss him. I tried to kiss him to tell him our whole love story, the way I grieved when I found he was dead, the way he meant the world to me and the way I ached for him.

He pressed his forehead against mine. There was a light, unnatural breeze. My eyes flashed open. He was gone. In an instant, I lost the colour from my face and felt as if the blood had run down into my shoes. I swayed for just a moment before Nina caught me and lowered me to the ground. I had no strength anymore. Time seemed to pass.

"Miss Chandran.. Sweetheart, open your eyes."

There were two voices, both familiar and unfamiliar calling my name. I stared up at the two faces. Nina held me and there was a woman in the cop attires kneeling next to her.

"Miss Chandran, my name is Chitra Arnasallam." she said. From her name, I could say she was brown as me. "Mr.Alex sent us to look for you kids. I'm sorry for whatever happened." she added.

Mr.Alex? Gustin's father... That striked me. "Does he know that..." I asked but then got interrupted. "Oh yes, Miss Chandran. He has come to Rockhurst." Tears escaped from the corner of my eyes. My head felt painful. "Sebastian! Come here!" she called out for another cop in there. In a quick and supple motion, Sebastian pulled me up from Nina's lap and into his arms. There seemed to be lights and deep babble of male voices. He slowed as he approached the commotion. "We're taking Miss Chandran, Parrish and Mr. Evans to the hospital. They're all hurt." he told somebody.

"What happened to Shini and Jacob? Where is my Gustin's body?" my mind wondered aloud.

There were lights everywhere. There were few reporters with cameras. It felt like a funeral procession. Sebastian walked, then placed me carefully in the ambulance. I could see Colton was already in it. He was unconscious. Sebastian waited for Nina to hop inside then closed the door. I closed my eyes.

IT BEGAN

AFTER ONE YEAR AND A HALF.

The Pebble Fall Theme Park was finally renovated and opened in Rockhurst, with a celebration featuring Valcano Party leaders, children's choir, Shrek and other fairy tale characters. This was the day I had been waiting for, the reopening ceremony of The Pebble Fall Theme Park. As for time, yes it did pass, even when each tick of the second hand ached like the pulse of blood behind a bruise. Colton and Nina were married. It was definitely too early to be married being barely 20, but after whatever happened that night in the theme park, they wanted to. They were not expecting any babies for now though. As for Shini and Jacob, they were in prison. Shini was semi – paralysed while Jacob was mentally ill. Deep inside, a part of me felt sorry for them but no, they actually deserved it. It was the taste of their own medicines after all. There hadn't been a day where I did not ache for him, Gustin. At first, Colton and Nina did not agree in the idea of renovating this place after the tragic experience which caused our nightmares. In spite of that, I insisted and firmly said that we ought to get The Pebble Fall Theme Park business construction done so that my beloved's death wouldn't be unjustified.

The former First Lady, Rita Barrack was invited to do the honors and cut the ribbon. There were reporters all over with cameras capturing the event. The First Lady was accompanied by Mr. Alex and I, followed by Colton and Nina. I was in a maroon long sleeved bubble print tea dress with my straight hair let drop. I had red lipstick over my lips. The crowd gave a huge round of applause after the ribbon was cut. I could see Colton and Nina shedding tears. A tear escaped from the corner of my eye. Mr. Alex patted my back as he smiled with glistering eyes. Suddenly, I felt a cool breeze on my neck.

"YOU'VE MADE IT, HONEY." I heard his voice whispering in my ear. I smiled, my eyes glassy. "Welcome to *THE PEBBLE FALL THEME PARK!*" the host of the event exclaimed. I sighed.

KEERTIGA, WHEN SHE WAS IN THE PROCESS OF
WRITING THE PEBBLE FALL THEME PARK IN THE END
OF 2016.

KEERTIGA, WITH BOTH OF HER FRIENDS, ZIA AND
SHINI (KEERTHURGAZIA) AFTER DISCUSSING IDEAS
IN THE LIBRARY.

THE PEBBLE FALL THEME PARK INITIAL COVER,
MADE BY ZIA FOR WATTPAD IN YEAR 2017.